The

Also by Mohammed Mrabet/Paul Bowles
and published by Peter Owen

Love With a Few Hairs
The Lemon
M'Hashish
Look and Move On

MOHAMMED MRABET

The Big Mirror

Taped and translated from the Moghrebi by
PAUL BOWLES

PETER OWEN · LONDON

ISBN 0 7206 0730 2

PETER OWEN PUBLISHERS
73 Kenway Road London SW5 0RE

First published in Great Britain 1989
© Mohammed ben Chaib el Hajjem 1977

Printed in Great Britain by Billings of Worcester

THE BIG MIRROR

1

A widow who lived in the town received a visit one afternoon from her nephew Ali.

The young man owned wide farmlands in the nearby hills.

The woman was sitting with the daughter of a neighbor when Ali came in. He kissed his aunt's forehead, and then he noticed the girl.

And his aunt saw his eyes grow wider as he looked at her.

This is Rachida, she said, and they sat together and talked.

Not much later the girl went out, and Ali was left alone with his aunt.

They discussed the girl. Is she married? Ali asked.

No.

And is she a virgin?

Yes, yes, his aunt said impatiently. Of course she is.

Ali was silent.

His aunt waited before she went on. Are you interested in her?

He frowned. I might be, and I might not be.

Why do you say that, son?

Too much beauty. It worries me. I feel she could be dangerous.

How can that be?

I know we say that only Allah can give and take life. But that kind of beauty could either keep a man alive or kill him.

His aunt did not seem to be listening. Yes, yes, son. A fine girl. An only child, the same as you. For understanding each other.

Maybe, said Ali. But she worries me.

His aunt laughed. A man afraid of a girl?

No, he said. Afraid of the beauty.

That night in his sleep while the owls called in the orchard Ali found that he was married.

His bride was the girl he had met at his aunt's house. This made him happy, but only at first. In the back of his mind he was afraid.

And watching her face closely, he saw it changing in form, little by little, growing into something evil, and he understood that he was with a witch.

He awoke in a sweat and stared into the darkness.

2

The men who worked for Ali on his farm were fond of him.

He thought of them as his friends, and often sat for hours talking with them after they had finished work.

But when he sat with them at breakfast the next morning in the garden, Ali was thoughtful, and as he drank his tea and ate his bread, he said nothing. At length one of the workers turned to him to ask if he felt ill.

Ali was hoping to clean his mind of the dark thoughts the dream had left there.

Without thinking he said: My aunt wants me to get married.

Your aunt? they said, surprised.

Then he told them the whole story. She wants to arrange the marriage for me, he added. But do I want to?

As Ali heard the men's voices urging him to marry, the dream seemed to go further away.

Yes, he said, first to himself and then aloud to them: Yes, perhaps I should.

That evening he went again to his aunt's house.

She kissed him and led him to an inner room where in the dimness he could see the seated figure of another woman.

As he moved toward her, he saw that it was the girl Rachida.

After he had greeted her, he turned to his aunt. What does she say? How does Rachida feel about it?

His aunt merely stood in the doorway, without speaking.

But the girl said: How do I feel about what?

About marrying me, said Ali.

She stood up, and like a sleepwalker moved toward him, her arms outstretched.

Ali turned to his aunt, but she had disappeared.

When the girl's hands touched his face, she burst into tears.

He drew her to him. Don't you want to be married? he whispered.

But she was not able to speak.

Tomorrow my parents will be at your house, Ali promised. He kissed her and went to look for his aunt, to tell her the news.

The following day Ali spent in the souqs,

buying robes and qaftans and gold jewelry.

Afterward he went to buy sweetmeats and pastries, and carried everything home to his parents so that they could start out for Rachida's father's house, taking the gifts along with them.

The older people sat down together. Rachida stood in the doorway, watching the parcels being opened.

Ali's parents began by saying that he was their only child. Finally they said: Name your figure. How much do you want?

They reached a price together, and then Ali's parents rose, presented their respects, and went home.

When Ali returned from the farm, his mother told him: It's all arranged.

The next day Ali made more purchases. Then, making certain that he had enough money with him, he went to meet Rachida's father.

Together they called for the notaries, and they all walked to Rachida's house.

The rooms were full of the laughter of many girls, Rachida's friends who were visiting her.

The men went into a room by themselves, where they were served a meal. When they had finished their tea the notaries began to fill out the papers.

They called for Rachida.
Do you want to marry this man?
Yes.

It was soon done. Ali paid the notaries their fee and handed over the sum agreed upon to Rachida's father.

At that moment the house was filled with the voices of the girls, who all cried: Yuyuyuyuyu!

As the notaries left, the girls began to sing and play their drums.

Ali now had to find a house in the city where he and Rachida could live. During the following days he looked at many of them, but only one seemed to him fine enough.

This house was ancient and vast. It had a series of dark high-ceilinged rooms around a huge courtyard.

He arranged to buy it, and hired a large squad of workers who could restore it quickly.

When they had finished, he filled the house with thick rugs and soft cushions and low tables, so that it was ready to be lived in.

The time for the wedding came. Ali celebrated his own feast in the new house, while Rachida's feast was held at her father's.

After the women and girls had danced and sung, Rachida was carried out and fitted into the almaria which was to take her to Ali.

They closed the almaria, put it on the back of a horse, and began to move through the streets. The oboists and drummers played fast music, the crowd carried torches, the women screamed, and the girls danced.

And the procession moved through the town to Ali's house.

In front of the door they lifted the almaria down from the horse. Quickly they carried it inside to a room where there was a great mirror that reached from the floor almost to the ceiling, and here they opened it and helped Rachida to get out.

She stood in the middle of the ballroom with its flickering candles, surrounded by all the girls. She saw her own reflection, standing in her white wedding gown, and she hurried over to the glass to examine herself.

As she flounced and danced before the mirror she began to laugh excitedly. All at once her laughter turned to sobbing.

The girls crowded around her, trying to comfort her, putting their arms around her and saying soothing words. But she paid them no heed. Only when Ali's arrival at the house caused all the girls to leave did she come to herself and stop crying.

Then Ali and Rachida stood side by side, wearing their white robes that shimmered in the candlelight.

He turned, murmuring her name, and slowly began to lift the filmy veil that covered her face.

She stared at him.

That mirror frightens me, she said. Have them take it out.

Yes, yes. Whatever you want.

They ate the meal that had been prepared for them, and spent a happy night together.

3

Early the following morning Ali collected some friends and went with them to the hammam. They spent the morning there bathing and wrestling.

During this time the parents of both the bride and groom arrived at the house to visit Rachida, bringing a black servant along with them. They looked for Rachida in her bedroom, but she was not there.

There was the sound of singing in another part of the house.

They opened the door of the ballroom.

Rachida stood in the center of the room, entirely naked, with only her long tresses to cover her, half of them falling in front and half behind.

They all remained quite still, staring at what they saw.

Then Rachida's mother cried: Is there something wrong with you?

Rachida looked at her mother and quickly put on her clothing. When she was dressed she said crossly: You knew I was in here. Why did you open the door? What do you want?

But what were you doing? insisted her mother.

You want to know what I was doing? I was enjoying being in Heaven. This room is Heaven to me because I can do as I like in it. And you come and push open the door without knocking or even calling out.

Yes, yes, they said. Now come out into the other room with us.

Then the women dressed Rachida in silk robes.

Groups of girls and women began to arrive, singing and pounding on drums. They started to dance as they came through the doorway.

When Ali returned from the hammam he found the house full of girls. He remembered that Rachida had asked him to have the mirror taken out of the ballroom. He spoke to the black servant about it, and she promised to call in some men to move it that afternoon.

No sooner had Ali gone out than the servant was given other work to do, so that she forgot about the mirror.

That evening when Ali returned he saw it still standing in its place. He mentioned it to Rachida, promising to have it taken out the next morning.

To his surprise she said: No! Leave it where it is. I need it.

Again Ali said, shrugging: Whatever you like.

The months went past, and the great mirror still stood in the ballroom. In the meantime Rachida had bought many others, so that the house was full of them. When he entered a room, Ali would see himself going through the doorway on the left and on the right, and as he walked along the corridors he would see his image at the far end, coming nearer. And every time he came into the house he would find Rachida in front of a mirror.

Habibi, he would say, what have you made in the kitchen for us today?

And she would always answer: Nothing. The black woman will do it.

But have you eaten?

I never have to eat, she would say. Looking into the glass is enough for me.

He would stare at her and shake his head.

One evening he went to visit her parents. As they talked, Ali suddenly said: The wedding was four months ago, and I have yet to see Rachida make even a glass of tea.

The old man wrung his hands.

My son, our daughter is not entirely well, he said. I think you know that. No need for me to tell you anything. You must decide whether you want to go on with her or not. If you want a divorce, she can come back here to us, but you must decide.

Ali found himself unable to answer the old man. Soon he said good night and went out.

As a result of his visit Rachida's mother

began to come every day to see her, and she also took charge of the kitchen and saw to it that Ali and Rachida ate regularly.

It did not take her long to see that Rachida was carrying a child.

As time went on, Rachida grew sad to see her body losing the beauty of its original form. She passed her days sitting naked in front of a mirror, weeping and complaining that she had grown ugly.

Ali spent more time with her, in the hope of distracting her. He would buy her new qaftans and necklaces, and then, without saying anything to her beforehand, pile the gifts on the cushions in front of the great mirror in the ballroom. Then, when he had lighted all the candles, he would take her hand and lead her inside to the mirror.

Rachida spent her days in the ballroom in the midst of piles of clothing, endlessly putting on and taking off the robes and trinkets that lay around her.

4

It was the day of the naming-feast for Ali's son, seven days after Rachida had given birth to him.

Ali and Rachida were in the ballroom. She stood before the big mirror smiling at herself, and he stood watching her.

All at once Ali had the feeling that a wave of sickness was breaking over him. He could not have said in what part of his body, or what kind of illness it was, since he had never felt such a thing before.

He said nothing, but he saw Rachida glance at him in the mirror, as if she already knew about it, and were merely waiting for him to mention it.

This was his first warning.

As time passed, Rachida's beauty returned, and she spent her time in front of the mirror without weeping and complaining. But she would have nothing to do with the baby. The entire care of him was given over to her mother, who moved into the house in order to be always on hand.

19

If Rachida's mother went out, she would leave the baby in charge of the black servant.

One Friday when the old woman had gone to the cemetery to lay myrtle on the family's graves, Rachida wandered into the kitchen. The black woman sat in the corner holding the baby.

Here, said Rachida, giving her some coins. I want you to go to the market and get me some melons.

The servant passed the baby to Rachida and went out.

Rachida carried the baby slowly through the house, until she stood in the ballroom.

She laid the baby on the floor, locked the doors, pulled the curtains across the windows, and lighted some candles. She looked into the glass and admired her bright red qaftan. This gave her the idea of wrapping the baby in a gown of the same color.

She held the baby in her arms and looked down at him. Then she looked at herself holding him.

Would his blood match the red dress? she said to herself.

And so she brought out a barber's razor, and, watching herself in the mirror every instant, she sliced the baby's neck from below one ear to below the other.

The blood ran out, and she rubbed her hands in it and held them beside the dress to compare the color.

She sat for a long time watching herself

play with the blood. Now and then she smiled at her reflection.

The servant came and knocked.

Here are your melons! she cried, but Rachida did not reply.

Somewhat later Ali returned and began to call out for Rachida.

When he pounded on the ballroom door, she fell onto the rug and lay still, leaving Ali no choice but to push against the door until finally the lock gave way.

He stepped into the room, to see Rachida, the baby and the razor all lying on the floor.

He saw that his son was dead. Then he looked at Rachida, and saw that she was alive.

She did not respond when he touched her. After he had fetched water and dashed it into her face, she opened her eyes and slowly sat up, staring at him.

Then she wiped her face with her sleeve and said angrily: Why did you throw water at me?

Rachida! Who did it? Who killed our baby?

Rachida seemed to be remembering.

The girl, she said, speaking as if she were asleep. The girl had the razor in her hand, and she cut the baby's neck.

Who? Where is she?

But then Ali recalled that the door had been locked. There was no one else in the ballroom.

He stared at the blood on Rachida's hands and face.

Then after a moment he turned and went out of the room.

He walked directly to the house of Rachida's parents, told them to follow him, and led them back to Rachida.

When they went into the room Rachida was sitting on a divan surrounded by candles, looking down at the floor where the baby still lay in a pool of blood beside the razor.

Allah! Allah! her mother cried. What have you done?

Rachida looked at her mother and shook her head.

Nothing, Mother. It was the other girl. You know the one. Come, if you want to see her.

Rachida's father and mother let her lead them to the big mirror.

There! she said, pointing.

Her mother gave a great cry, and began to sob.

My girl has gone mad!

Rachida's father was staring open-eyed into the mirror, not believing what he saw. Rachida stood between him and his wife, pointing at herself. But instead of the red qaftan, the reflection showed her wearing the shining white gown of a bride.

Rachida smiled when she saw her parents' consternation.

You see her? she said, and she began to

laugh.

In the mirror they saw the girl in white weeping silently.

Ali turned away. The skin on his body prickled with gooseflesh, because he was facing something beyond his understanding.

When night came they wrapped the baby and carried it in secret outside the walls of the city and buried it on a rocky hillside.

It was evening by the time they all got back to the house. Ali still felt ill, and would have preferred not to be alone with Rachida. But as soon as they were inside, she motioned him to leave their parents and follow her into the ballroom.

She shut the door and they sat down.

It seems wrong that I should be the only sick one in a healthy family, she said. But Allah must have wanted it that way, and so he made me beautiful. And I caught the disease at the mirror. The best thing would be if I could die now, quickly. But everything comes from Allah.

She began quietly to sob, and Ali moved to take her in his arms.

As he did so, he glanced into the mirror, and saw the girl with Rachida's face hiding a sly grin. Then she began to shake with laughter.

Swiftly he looked down at Rachida herself. She was still sobbing, and her cheeks were wet with tears.

Ali felt the hairs bristle at the back of his

head.

Stop! Stop it! he cried, and he shook Rachida violently.

Little by little she grew calm. Only after that did Ali dare to glance again into the mirror.

This time he saw only himself with his arm around Rachida. The other girl had gone.

Rachida's parents took her home to sleep that night, leaving Ali alone in the house.

He lay in his bed unable to sleep, thinking of Rachida, the dead baby, and the mirror. He sweated and turned, and stared into the dark.

Late in the night he rose and tiptoed into the ballroom. Holding a feeble lamp, he gazed into the mirror.

Behind him in the shadows of the background, it seemed to him that he saw a figure stir. He swung around, but there was no one else in the room. Again he looked into the glass. The figure had come nearer to him, and he saw that it was wearing white robes. He recognized Rachida. She was in the mirror, but not in the room. At the same time she was lying asleep in her father's house.

Quickly he slipped out into the courtyard and shut the door behind him. He returned to his bed, but his mind was so crowded with thoughts about the mirror that he could not find his way to the place of sleep.

Early in the morning Ali set out for the farm. The day was bright and sunny, but he carried a cloud inside his head. He had not felt well since the day of the naming-feast, and now he felt very ill.

At the farm he called all the workers in from the fields, saying he wanted to talk to them. When they had assembled around him under the trees, he began to speak.

If for some reason you fail to see me here, remember that you work only for me. Whether I am here or not, you must go on as always, selling, buying and paying yourselves your own wages. What you have left over will go to my father. And may Allah keep you.

He dismissed the men and went to a small cabin that stood in the orchard.

It was very quiet inside. Ali stretched out on the cabin floor and fell into a deep sleep.

5

As he lay there sleeping, Ali began to see himself in a place where there were no trees or plants —only rocks, with water running between them. And he strode through the water, and saw himself come finally to a wide river.

He saw himself plunge into the water, and he watched his struggles against the current as he swam.

And as he looked at himself climbing up onto the other bank, he reached out his arms to seize the rocks, and he realized that he was wet. He scaled the rocks and went down the other side.

As he continued to walk, the boulders grew hot, and steam shot out of hidden places. He hurried ahead, hoping to reach a cooler spot. Soon he was running. His wet clothing hung heavily on him, and he could not draw enough breath.

He pulled off all his clothing and went on running between the hot boulders, his thirst growing by the minute. The steam poured out in clouds from behind the rocks. He slipped and fell to the ground.

As he looked up, it seemed to him that he saw Rachida approaching through the stream. Then he realized that it was the Rachida of the mirror, still dressed in white.

When she stood above him she smiled and greeted him.

Ali could say only one word: Water.

If I brought you some, would you be my husband?

Water!

You agree?

Yes! he cried. I swear by Allah.

She brought him water. He drank it slowly and poured it over himself. Then he lay back and rested for a while.

He looked up at the girl. She was not disturbed by his nakedness, but stood watching him.

Then he sat up and thanked her.

Good bye, she said. Keep walking in the direction you were going. You can get there.

When she had gone, he got up and walked on.

Very soon he came to an oasis. In the shade of the palms grew fruit trees, and water gurgled in the channels. A cool soft breeze stirred the air beneath the branches.

Ali sat down, leaning back against the trunk of a palm. As he began to doze, it seemed to him that he heard a voice calling his name.

He opened his eyes. It was hot in the cabin,

and he was bathed in sweat. One of his farmhands stood in the doorway.

There are some people who want to see you.

Ali stood up and stretched.

Outside under the trees, not far from the cabin, he saw a man and a woman.

As he approached them he wondered if perhaps they had known him when he was a boy.

Your name is Ali? the man said.

Who are you? said Ali, still trying to remember them.

The man went on. And your wife's name is Rachida?

Ali did not answer.

Then the woman spoke up. And yesterday she killed her baby?

Terrified, Ali opened his mouth to speak, but the man went on. And a few minutes ago you were a long way from here.

No! I was here in the cabin.

He pointed to the door and invited them to go inside. There he gave them each a mug of buttermilk.

No, he said again. I was on that mat asleep.

Your body was, perhaps, said the man. But where were you?

Ali saw that he must tell them his dream.

When he had finished, the man said: And you still have no idea who we are? The girl you promised to marry is our daughter.

29

Who else could we be? said the woman. My daughter is very much in love with you, and we wanted to see what sort of man you were. I think you could be happy together.

You understand, of course, said the man as they got up to go, we would have preferred to see her married to a living man rather than a dead one, but since she seems to want only you, we shall agree to the marriage. You may not always be dead.

Ali was too astonished to reply.

They bowed and went out.

Ali remained sitting where he was, feeling very uncomfortable. Their words had been so unlikely that he began to think the couple only a part of his dream.

He jumped up and ran outside, where he peered in all directions, but the couple was not in sight. He called to the farmhand who had come to announce their arrival.

Which way did they go, those people? he asked him.

They went into the cabin with you. After that, I don't know.

Ali thanked him and went inside, where he began to walk back and forth.

This is going to drive me out of my mind, he said to himself. But perhaps it already has, and all this is part of the sickness.

He slammed the cabin door and set out for the city. What had been a cloud in his head that morning was now a storm.

6

As soon as he stepped inside the house he heard Rachida's wailing. He stood in the dark corridor listening. The cries sounded like those of an animal or a demon. He felt his skin moving, and the hair on his head growing stiff.

Suddenly he was angry. He walked to the ballroom door and opened it.

As usual Rachida lay on a divan. He called her name very loud, startling her, so that she looked up at him.

Then she surprised him by bursting into rapid speech.

Why do you look like that, Ali? What is it? Are you sick? Are you dead?

Ali paid no heed to her words.

Rachida, I want to know. Why are you crying?

Because time is going by and the world is changing every instant. Whatever is conceived is born, and whatever is born dies. Nothing stays behind.

31

Then she jumped up.

I have some things for you, she told him. Here are two robes, one red and the other red and white. I knew what would look best on you, and I had to hunt for the colors I wanted.

Ali wanted to thank her, but she went on talking.

It frightens me to look at you these days, Ali. I suppose you realize how great the change is. No one would know you were the same man as before.

Nonsense!

Go and look at yourself in the glass, she said.

Ali walked over to the big mirror. Nothing but the room was reflected in it. Rachida came and stood beside him. He saw her clearly, but she was standing there alone.

This is impossible! Rachida cried. Where are you?

Ali turned and threw himself onto the couch. He leaned back and looked at the ceiling, muttering: Impossible. Yes. Impossible.

Rachida stood watching him. Presently she touched his arm.

Get up and try on the red robe, she said.

When he returned to the couch wearing the robe, she looked at him approvingly, ran her hand over his face, and began to give him tender kisses.

Then she drew back, looked again at him, and shook her head.

Ali! Ali! What a shame! Your color is ugly
with that red. Wait!

She got up and disappeared into another
part of the ballroom. Ali shut his eyes. He heard her
moving around. Then for a while there was silence.

Suddenly he heard Rachida's voice cry, as
if from another room: Get away from him!

His eyes flew open. Rachida was bending
over him. She held a barber's razor close to his throat,
but her head was already turning to look into the
mirror where the voice had come from.

He sprang up, trembling, and Rachida
dropped the razor. He stooped, seized it, and left the
room.

7

Ali sat by himself for a long time thinking about Rachida's illness and the trouble that could come as a result of it. And he marvelled at the voice from inside the mirror that had called out at the moment when he was in danger. Now and then he believed that all this was still a part of the dream he had started in the cabin at the farm. It occurred to him that perhaps the reason why Rachida had not cut his throat was that he was already dead, as the man and the woman had told him.

At length he glanced up. Rachida stood in the doorway, looking at him timidly.

When she saw that he had noticed her, she walked over to him.

Forgive me, Ali.

Of course I forgive you, he said. I forgive my wife. I love you. I would, even if you had cut my throat.

She gave him a radiant smile, and he felt the same dizziness as always when he saw it. For she was very beautiful, and when she smiled she became still more beautiful.

Ali, she said. Whatever I do, I hope you will understand.

What does that mean? he said with suspicion.

Rachida smiled again.

Just looking at your face when it goes pale like that makes me feel capable of doing anything, no matter what, she said softly.

Ali seized her shoulder. What are you trying to say, Rachida?

She drew away and looked down. Red on red, she said finally. Red blood on red silk. But better on white. Yes. Everyone understands that.

As she spoke, her eyes grew wider. Sheer white cloth with red blood on it! Like nothing else in the world!

Rachida, he said, shaking her. Rachida, your mind is wandering.

She stared at him. Your color at this moment is ghastly, hideous. It would make anyone sick just to see you. Your flesh is dark yellow. It looks as if it had earth inside it. What a pity, Ali.

Rachida! Stop talking! Let me speak.

Yes, she went on. My mind is going. True. A pity, Ali, a pity. What can I do?

She burst into tears and broke away from him. He heard her rush down the corridor into the ballroom and shut the door. He sat where he was for

36

a long time, listening to her cries. Then he rose and went to comfort her. But she did not seem to be aware of his presence, and merely continued to wail and sob.

This time Rachida's weeping went on all night. Ali lay awake, hearing it. Just before dawn she became quiet.

When the sun came up Ali got out of bed, washed, and stepped out into the street. Soon he met Rachida's mother walking with a neighbor woman.

How is Rachida? she asked him.

She cried all night, he said, waving his arms. This is enough! No more for me!

The other woman spoke up. You must bear it, my son.

Yes, he said. Go into the house and stay with her until I come back.

8

As Ali neared the end of his street, he came to a large group of men crowding in front of a house. He stopped and exchanged greetings with a neighbor whom he knew.

Has something happened?

They found a man in there with his throat cut. His family say they heard howling all night, and when it stopped, just before daybreak, the man began to scream. His wife thinks she saw a dark bird flying away from the window. She thinks it was an owl. The man was covered with blood, and his throat was open from one ear to the other.

A bird is not going to slit a man's throat, Ali said.

No one understands it. But they say it did. And this thing howled all night.

Ali nodded and went on his way, taking long steps. He began to sweat and his face grew pale, and as he walked along he found himself trembling.

When he got to his farm the men working in the orchard greeted him. He did not reply, even when they called again to him. He walked straight to the cabin, stepped inside, and shut the door.

Sitting there alone and considering the events, Ali became convinced that Rachida, not having managed to cut his throat, had killed another man in his place. And he believed that it was only the cry from the girl in the mirror that had saved him. At the same time both ideas were absurd.

Rachida was his wife, and because he loved her he could not bear to admit that she was growing worse.

Then he remembered that with the sickness of beauty what is unreal seems the same as what is real. He had the disease, and it made him feel that he was at the edge of evil. He began to sob.

Now and then he groaned, and some of his workmen passing near the cabin heard him. They stopped and called out to him.

Go on with your work, he told them. Just leave me by myself. I know everything you could say. And the greatest favor you can do for me is not to say anything.

The men shrugged and went on with their work. Ali sat without stirring, feeling that the dark mouth of sickness was nearby, ready to swallow him. Sometimes it seemed so near that he could feel it pulling at him.

An image floated in his mind, that of a

white cloth stained with red. As he studied it, a great wave of happiness suddenly swept through him.

Yes, he murmured, white muslin and blood. Rachida was right. Like silk and honey.

A strange excitement seized him, leaving him weak, as if a moment ago his blood had been dark, and now suddenly had turned watery. And in his head passed a procession of bloodstained cloths.

Then he burst into loud laughter, jumped up, and went out of the cabin.

It was already night. As he walked down the lane he was still laughing. The night watchmen saw him going, and shook their heads.

Poor Ali, they said.

9

At home Rachida's mother was indignant that Ali should be coming in so late.

Where have you been?

Sleeping. There was no sleep last night, and tonight it will be the same.

I was only waiting until you came, she said quickly. Now I must go home.

No, said Ali. You must stay here.

Rachida heard this, and appeared from the courtyard.

Why should she stay here? she demanded.

To humor her, Ali said: I thought she might like to hear about white and red.

Yes! cried Rachida. She rushed over to her mother and began to stroke her cheeks. White and red are lovely together, Mother. You must have been very beautiful when you were young.

She undid a kerchief that was tied under her mother's chin, and ran her hands softly over her throat. Then she hugged her.

Her mother patted her on the shoulder. Well, things change and time passes, she said. If we're to sleep here, we must eat now.

When dinner was over and the two older women had gone to bed, Rachida wandered into the ballroom. A few minutes later Ali appeared, turning to look into the big mirror as he passed it.

Once again the glass gave him no reflection of himself. He walked quickly by, hoping that Rachida had noticed nothing.

It seemed to him that he could feel the sickness closing over him more firmly at each moment. He found himself thinking: To become a bird. Yes. If only I could! That would be the greatest pleasure of all.

As if he had spoken aloud, Rachida turned to him.

No use, Ali, she said, shaking her head. Not many people can cry all night long. The day goes past little by little. The night stays without moving, full of voices. Allah made the night first. Give up the idea. Because, Ali, there are other birds.

She picked up a bright red qaftan and slipped into it. As she glanced into the mirror she cried out. Then she began to shout at her reflection.

What are you waiting for in there?

Then in a very different voice that seemed to come from behind the mirror she went on: Yes, you look lovely tonight, Rachida. Lovely with a kind of beauty that no one else was given, and that no one

44

can reach. Still, you are leaving, and Ali is staying behind with me.

That will be only when I've finished with him! cried Rachida.

Whatever you can do to him will be better than having him swallowed up by your sickness. Anything but becoming like you! the other voice replied.

With this Rachida let herself slide to the floor, where she threw her body in all directions and screamed.

Ali tried to calm her, but as usual she paid him no attention.

The noise woke her mother and the other woman, and they came together to the ballroom and talked to her, all to no avail.

Come, said Ali to the two women, and they went out of the room and shut the door.

Now, he said. We must sit here and wait for morning. No one must fall asleep, even for an instant. We must keep our eyes open as long as the sky is dark.

But why? cried Rachida's mother.

Ali did not reply.

They sat for hour after hour, listening to Rachida's cries and lamentations.

Just before dawn she stopped, and there was only silence.

Ali leapt to his feet and hurried to the ballroom door. He put his hand on the knob. Fear seized him. He shivered and walked back to the place where he had been sitting.

When the sun came up he stepped out of the house into the bright street. And then the sounds of many women wailing reached his ears. He turned to a man standing nearby and asked him what was wrong.

Ah, sidi, a brother of mine is dead. No one can understand it. Asleep in bed with his wife, and his throat cut with a razor. She says that when she woke up there was this huge bird that had lighted on him. She says it had a razor in its claw.

Impossible!

She began to scream, but the bird had already run the blade across his throat. Then it dropped the razor and went out through the window.

You mean you kept the razor? Ali asked him.

Yes, I have it, said the man.

Would you mind letting me see it? Ali asked him.

The man brought the razor and handed it to Ali.

He looked at it. It was the razor he had hidden after Rachida's attack on him.

Very strange, Ali murmured.

Something else, the man continued. My brother's wife says the bird flew from their window straight to your house. It may be in there now.

Could you let me keep the razor for a while?

Yes. Be careful.

Ali turned around and went back into his house.

Rachida was asleep on the divan in the ballroom. The heavy red curtains were drawn and the room was nearly dark.

To be absolutely certain, he went directly to the shelf where he had put the razor. As he had expected, the shelf was empty.

He tiptoed over to where Rachida lay and stood for a while looking down at her. The sheet that covered her had a few smears of blood on it. As he stared at the bloodstains he felt himself grinning. Then he laughed aloud, and Rachida opened her eyes.

What is it? she demanded.

Ali continued to laugh, and in a way particularly offensive to Rachida. When she had had enough of it, she sprang at him without warning, clawing at his neck with her fingernails. He pushed her violently and she fell to the floor.

He stood rubbing his hand over his throat, where the blood was trickling in several places. He looked at his fingers, and knelt above Rachida, smearing the blood over her cheeks, never ceasing to laugh.

Our neighbor is dead, Rachida, he whispered. Killed by a bird. With a razor.

Rachida sat up. She seemed not to have heard him.

Ali, she said. Your blood has a very delicate flavor. Straight from your neck. It tastes like honey. But I got so little of it! I should have had more. And when I've finished with sickness and gone on my way, you can have that one waiting behind the glass. If you can believe she's alive and real like me, maybe you can be happy with her.

But Rachida, he said, I want to be happy with you, not with her. Remember, I have the disease too. Perhaps we could be happy together. I tell you, I understand red on white. I enjoy white cheeks with blood on them. I'm happy when night comes down, and I hear something that sounds like a nightingale singing. A very sweet, small voice weeping.

Rachida stared at him doubtfully, since this was the opposite of what he usually told her. Ali went on.

And as I listen to that voice I can feel myself turning into an angel. And that is when I want to see blood running down your cheeks.

Yes, she said. My cheeks will be colored red, and I think it will be soon. And the day will be like no other day, like nothing even in dreams. The affarit and the djenoun will kneel in prayer. Lightning and thunder! Rain pouring down, drowning all the animals, caving in the houses. And you, Ali, balanced between the sky and the earth. If the hair breaks, you fall and are lost. If the hair bends and lets you down little by little, until your feet touch the ground, then you have freedom. It will be a day not to forget.

I expect to be here, said Ali. If not, I can

see it afterward.

I have nothing more to say, Rachida declared. Whatever is finished is dead, and so I forgive you.

She settled herself on the rug, as if to sleep, and Ali went out into the street.

10

Ali had not gone very far before he overtook a funeral procession. The murdered neighbor was being carried to the cemetery.

Catching sight of the man's brother, Ali began to walk beside him.

Thank you for lending me this, he said, handing him the razor.

They walked along with the procession.

The body on the litter was wrapped in a length of white muslin. Here and there Ali could see blood slowly staining the cloth. The sight made his head swim and his heart leap ahead.

The people passed into the cemetery and the bearers set the litter on the ground. A moment later the body was lowered into the grave.

Earth was shoveled over it, the tolba chanted, and finally everyone went away. Ali, however, slipped off and contrived to stay behind in the cemetery after they had gone.

He went to the grave and sat staring at it,

silent and motionless. The birds in the trees sang for a while.

Night fell, and an owl flew down and lighted among the graves. From time to time it cried out. Frogs began to croak not far away. The sky grew very bright and the moon rose, perfectly full.

At length, his heart pounding, Ali took up a shovel and set to work digging up the earth that covered the body. The owl was startled and flew off.

When he had uncovered the corpse, he quickly pulled away all the cloth that was wrapped around it. Much of it was soaked with blood. Then he saw the slash across the man's throat from one ear to the other, shining in the moonlight.

He shoveled the earth back over the body, rolled up the length of cloth, stuffed it under his arm, and walked out of the graveyard.

When he got home he found Rachida sitting with her mother and the neighbor woman. Where have you been all this time? they demanded.

Living with white and red, he said, looking at Rachida. With red and white.

Rachida opened her eyes wide. Allah! Allah! she cried. I already feel better, just seeing you come in. Tell me everything.

Later. I want to eat now.

When the meal was over, Rachida's mother said: Now I really must go home.

At this hour, Mother? No. Stay and sleep here.

Ali spoke up. Yes. Go and sleep in the other room.

The two women looked at each other and shrugged. They said good-night and went into their room, bolting the door firmly. And they continued to stare at each other.

What can we do? said Rachida's mother finally. We need sleep badly, and those two maniacs are out there. What are they saying, and what are they planning to do?

The other woman yawned. The best thing is to go to sleep.

When they had been alone for a few minutes, Ali turned to Rachida. Get up. Come into the sala. I have something interesting to show you.

Rachida followed him into the ballroom and he shut the door. After he had lighted the candles, he tossed her the cloth. She unfolded it to examine the great stains of blood, and spread it out on top of the rug. Then she lay down on it, heaved a sigh, and smiled.

At last life is becoming what it should be, she murmured. The greatest works of art are done in red and white. The colors of a world where even the farthest things can be seen. A world that has never been touched! Where did you get the cloth, Ali?

I think you know where it comes from, because it belongs to you, he told her.

She sat up. Did you take it out of his grave?

Yes, I did. I waited there until dark, and took it by moonlight. And I saw the way his neck had been carved. Marvellous, Rachida! So easy with a good razor. Red on white. Beautiful, yes. But very expensive.

Rachida was growing more excited. Yes, Ali! Blood is priceless. No price they can put on it is high enough. Terribly expensive, yes, but so good! And so sweet, added Ali. Sweet, Rachida.

She was quiet for a moment. Then she said: It's a pity I never had yours, never had it to drink or play with. All I've done is taste it.

I could have had yours, he told her. Perhaps I should have taken it. I left it up to you to do everything. But you came late and your work was clumsy. You had no time.

The blood helps you to feel better for a while, she said. But no matter how much of it you drink, it will never cure the disease, nor will any doctor you can find. Nor any fqih. You have it, Ali. Perhaps you think that because your doctor always comes dressed as a bride, she will be able to help you. Maybe she will. Who knows?

Ali had ceased to listen.

Rachida, he said, and kissed her. She returned his kisses.

Together they sank to the floor where the bloody cloth was spread, and there they remained all night long making love.

In the morning when they awoke and looked

54

at each other, they smiled.

Allah! Rachida exclaimed. To sleep on a winding-sheet still soaked with fresh blood! What luxury!

Last night I had a nightmare, he told her. I was in Gehennem. It was hot, hot! I was lying there burning to death, and suddenly you were there standing over me. And when I begged you for a little water, you pointed at me and laughed.

Rachida was thoughtful. I dreamed too, she said. I remember being half buried in the sand. It was somewhere in the Sahara, and there was a terrible sun, stronger than the sun is in our world. And you came walking toward me naked, and you pulled me out of the sand and carried me to a place where there was water running into a pool, and we bathed together in the shade of the trees. And it was then that I saw blood running from you and dripping into the water. Red in water! Water turning red! After a while the blood stopped running from you and you caught fire. The flames crackled like guns, and the sound made me feel light and happy. I don't know why. The flames grew higher, and I could feel myself going up into the air with them. Then I opened my eyes, and we were both here, lying on red and white. I was glad, and so I smiled.

If only every night could be like last night, we could rest, said Ali. And in his head he added: And not have to lie awake listening for the moment when you stop crying and go out to cut someone's throat.

He sighed. You remember when I was happy and healthy like any other man, and could walk in the street without being ashamed? Those days are finished, because I picked the wrong wife. I chose the sick one, and here I am, sick the same as she is.

Yes! said Rachida angrily. And I hope you get worse. I want to see you in the same state I'm in now.

Ali laughed. We could cry together all night, and sing mouwaals while we cry.

All night, Ali, you know. All night long.

There was a knock at the door. Quickly Ali hid the spotted cloth. Rachida's mother had come to say that breakfast was ready.

11

Ali spent the day at the farm. The hours of fresh air and sunshine helped him, so that at twilight when he started out for the town he was in good spirits. But as he entered the house he heard Rachida's wailing.

The two older women huddled in a corner of the kitchen, waiting anxiously for him.

She has an old cloth covered with blood that she keeps kissing, said her mother. And screaming all day. I locked her into the sala to keep her out of trouble. But we're both very tired.

Give me the key, Ali said, and she handed it to him. Then he went and dressed himself in white.

He unlocked the ballroom door. Rachida! he called.

Rachida opened her eyes. Seeing him all in white, she rose from the floor where she had been lying, and laughing in the midst of her tears, she began to run her hands over his garments.

Ali, this is the night! she babbled. The night without end!

Listen, Rachida. Listen to me! I have something to tell you. I'm going to tie you up. I'm going to bind your arms and legs, and leave you that way, so that nothing will happen. And tonight will be quiet.

He seized her and bound her hands behind her, and wound the rope around her legs and tied it tight. Then he went out of the room and locked the door behind him, leaving her screaming alone in the ballroom.

While he was eating his dinner the screams stopped, and he ate the last part of his meal in silence.

He called to the women: She's gone to sleep.

Afterward, he tiptoed to the ballroom door, knelt down, and put his eye to the keyhole. What he saw was so unlikely that once again he decided he was asleep.

The room seemed to be full of old women. They were clustered around Rachida, who still lay on thet floor. He counted seven of them.

The sight of these hags swarming around his wife filled him with terror and disgust, and finally with fury. Before he realized what was happening, they had cut the ropes that bound her.

Rachida sprang up, and at that moment they all seemed to be shrinking and growing darker. They moved in a strange manner along the floor. Then he saw that instead of faces they had the heads and beaks of birds. All at once they rushed to the

58

windows and flew off, one after the other.

Ali stood up and wiped away the sweat that trickled down his face. Then he walked back into the room where the two women sat.

Is she asleep? asked Rachida's mother.

I think so, he said.

He sat down and shut his eyes. He felt cold.

The two women said good night and retired to their bedroom.

It was nearly two hours later when Ali got up and returned to peer through the keyhole in the ballroom door.

At first he could see nothing. There seemed to be less light in the room than there had been before.

Then Rachida came into view, and he realized that there were others with her. The old women were back.

He stood up and began to walk along the corridor, not knowing what to believe, or what to do. As he stepped into the dark courtyard, he heard his name pronounced clearly by a girl's voice, faint but very close to him, like an insect buzzing in his ear.

He put his hand to his ear and glanced quickly behind him.

Go on talking, he said aloud. I can stand it. Nothing is real, in any case.

The voice was saying: You must sleep. Go to bed and rest. Nothing will happen. I shall be there.

Without thinking, he answered. Thank you.

That would be wonderful.

A great wave of sleepiness had come over him. He went to his room and fell asleep, and slept soundly all the rest of the night.

By the time he awoke, Rachida and the two women were eating their breakfast. He sat down and ate with them, avoiding Rachida's glance and addressing himself only to her mother.

Today I must go home, she declared. I can come by tomorrow, incha'Allah.

As you like, Ali said. Ouakha.

He took leave of them and set out for the farm.

Shortly afterward the two older women gathered up their things and went out, leaving Rachida alone in the house.

12

For a time Rachida strolled back and forth under the orange trees in the patio. Then she turned and went into the ballroom. She shut and locked all the doors, and drew the curtains so that the room was very dim.

After she had lighted several candles and placed them around the mirror, she carefully spread a clean white cloth on the floor not far away.

Standing before the mirror, she began to try on her gilt and brocaded garments. Qaftans, zigdouns, djellabas and robes, one after the other.

She brought cushions and piled them in front of the mirror, and leaned back on them to admire herself. The clothes were scattered everywhere in the room, and still she brought out more. In this way she passed the entire day.

When dusk arrived, the only light came from the candles. Wearing a white gown, she sat before the mirror and began to comb her hair. Then she stood up and went on combing. The hair reached down to her thighs, but it seemed to her that it was longer on the left side than on the right.

Taking a long razor and looking always into the glass, she cut a little hair from the bottom, and stepped back to see it better.

Then she frowned and cut some from the other side. This did not suit her, either.

She continued to cut, a little at a time, here and there, trying to make it look as attractive as it had been before she had started cutting it. Finally, in a fury at what she had done, she began to hack at her hair from all sides, and it dropped in a mass on the floor.

Without her hair she looked like a shorn sheep. She stared at what she saw in the glass, and took up a second razor from the table. Then with a razor in each hand, watching her face in the mirror, she made a gash in each cheek.

At the sight of the blood springing from the white flesh, she gave a long cry of delight.

Then, intent on the picture she saw in the mirror, she made more gashes in her face. More blood appeared, and she burst into triumphant laughter.

With the need to destroy what she saw in the glass, she continued to slash at her face and throat. Pieces of flesh fell from her cheeks. Her hands moved lower, and she sliced her breasts, and soon she slid to the floor, onto the white cloth, where she lay still. From time to time she made a feeble sound which might have been laughter.

Ali, returning from the farm, came into the house and tried all the doors into the ballroom.

He listened, and heard nothing.

He called Rachida's name, and got no reply.

When he had battered in one of the doors, he stepped inside and saw Rachida lying on the white cloth, her blood coloring it red. Nothing of her face remained, neither eyes nor nose nor lips nor cheeks. Everything had become a mass of meat and blood.

Yet she was there. And he called to her.

Rachida! Rachida. Where is the red and white? Everything is red. Why, Rachida, why?

He stood over her, rubbing his face with his hands as he sobbed.

You've gone, he murmured. You've left me alone. Now you can rest, and I can be the one to suffer. Alone in this house without you.

Presently he pulled the bloody cloth out from under Rachida and hid it away where no one would be likely to find it. Then he went out of the ballroom and locked the door behind him.

He hurried to the house where Rachida's parents lived.

Come with me, he told them.

They looked at his face. What is it, Ali?

Finished. Over. Gone! he sobbed.

They stared at him.

Alone! She's dead.

Rachida's mother shrieked. They rushed out

of the house, and through the streets, Ali following behind them. At his house, he unlocked the door.

When they came to the ballroom, Ali slipped in ahead of the old couple, crying: Wait!

And he brought out a large blanket and spread it over Rachida, completely covering her.

They had to force Rachida's mother to go into another room, where she wept and tore at her clothing and hair.

Then Ali returned to the ballroom and stood before the mirror. The reflection he saw was of a man who looked like him, but who was dressed differently, and all in black.

So it still goes on, he said to himself.

He went back to Rachida's mother, and tried to soothe her.

She's gone, nothing more, he said. Death is part of life, and not something to weep about. You know Moslems are forbidden to mourn. The thing now is to decide what has to be done.

Rachida's father shook his head helplessly.

Sleep here tonight, Ali went on. You were afraid before, because of Rachida. But now?

They let Ali persuade them. He settled them in a bedroom, said good night, and left them. Then he locked himself into the ballroom, where he spread out the length of white cloth stained with Rachida's blood, and lay down to sleep on the floor beside her, using her body as a pillow. He dreamed that the night smelled of jasmin and mint.

13

In the morning the house was filled with relatives. They crowded around the body in the ballroom, not daring to lift the black blanket that covered it.

At length a litter was brought, and without being washed or wrapped in a kfin, Rachida was borne out of the house through the streets to the cemetery.

The burial took place near a cypress tree. The workmen covered the body with earth and filled in the grave, and the families slowly went out of the cemetery.

Ali stayed behind, sitting on the ground near the grave, thinking of Rachida, and sobbing quietly.

Night came, and the moon was still very large and bright. There were tuberoses lying at the head of the grave, and carnations lay at the foot. The flowers in the moonlight had no color, only scent.

And as he sat looking at the grave, he realized that smoke was rising slowly from the earth that covered it. The idea that even now Rachida was not free from the disease, that she was still somehow involved in her games with the enemy, struck him as unbearable.

He leapt to his feet and began to search frantically for a shovel that might have been left behind by one of the gravediggers. This time, however, they had been more careful. When he went back to the cypress tree, not only was there no more sign of smoke, but he was unable even to find the place where the grave had been.

Rather than allowing these things to startle him, Ali told himself that they were merely symptoms of the disease.

He walked back to the empty house, and went into the ballroom. Without looking into the mirror, he lay down in front of it. Rachida had sat here day after day, and she had bled to death in the very spot where he was lying. He saw the tuberoses and the smoke in the moonlight.

Not even the grave was real, he said to himself.

He lay for a long time without stirring, deep in his thoughts, until at last he fell asleep.

The next morning as he was having breakfast in the kitchen he began once more to think about the voice he had heard in his ear. It had been a soft voice, the voice of a girl.

This disease puts voices in your ear, he said to himself. If you can hear the voices, why should they not be able to hear you?

He waited, then called: Can you hear me?

He listened for a moment. Soon he heard the thin sound of the voice, very close to his ear.

Yes, Ali.

He looked up, and seeing no one, said: Ah, you did hear me.

Yes, but can you hear me? If you hear, and want to save yourself, listen to what I say. The only way for you to be cured is with the blood of the ones who ruined Rachida.

Yes, said Ali. His heart had begun to beat faster.

You must find them quickly, before they hear about Rachida's death. You must go out and walk in the street, all over the city. Whenever we come to one of them, I can point her out to you. I know them all.

As Ali stepped out into the street, the voice said: Just walk, and look at all the old women.

He walked to the middle of the city, through the market and the souqs.

Under the archway! said the voice. The one selling charcoal.

Ali approached the old woman, saying: Excuse me, lalla. My wife Rachida would like to see you tonight. And he gave her the time and the address and told her to be sure and come.

The old woman showed astonishment, but replied that since the gentleman's wife wished it, she would surely go to the house.

He walked on through the Saqqaya until he came to the bread market. There the voice suddenly said: The woman at the end of the row, with the grey litham over her face.

Ali leaned over to speak to the woman. She too seemed surprised by his invitation, but she also agreed to visit the house at the appointed hour.

He found two more in Bou Araqia, and the rest in other parts of the town. Each time the voice identified one of them for him, he would go up to her and deliver his message, and then carefully explain to her how to reach the house.

To him they looked like any other old women, but he let the voice guide him.

On his way home, Ali heard the voice say: You could spread out a white cloth, and bleed them to death, and pour the blood over you, standing on the cloth. That would make a good design, and give you great pleasure.

Ali did not reply, but he began to think about it, and said to himself: I could collect the blood in a big basin.

When he got to the house he set to work in the ballroom, preparing it for the evening.

He thought the voice had gone, but he realized that it was still with him when, as he unfolded the white cloth and spread it out on the floor, it suddenly spoke again.

Put it nearer to the mirror, it told him. You can take off your clothes and sit naked on the cloth and pour the blood over you.

Yes, Ali said. Lightning and thunder, wind and rain, and I'll be standing with a razor in my hand, laughing.

He brought in a great copper cauldron and set it on the white cloth. When he had completed all the preparations for the evening, he bathed and dressed in white.

He stopped in front of the glass to examine himself, and laughed when he saw his garments reflected in black.

As he stood there watching himself laugh, there was a faint knocking at the door. He went to open it, and found one of the old women.

Welcome! he said. Come in.

He led her to the ballroom, which was ablaze with lighted candles. As she passed from the dark corridor into the bright room, he reached around her neck from behind and thrust a bundle of cloth into her mouth, so that she could not make any sound. Then he bound her legs together and tied her hands behind her, carried her across the room, and propped her between two cushions, in such a way that she seemed to be sitting quietly. As the next one arrived, he followed the same procedure, setting her upright beside the first.

In the end, all seven of the crones sat on the

mtarrba, unable to move or make a sound.

He seized one of them, forced her to her knees, and bent her head over the edge of the cauldron. Then he slit her throat, letting the blood collect at the bottom.

When no more blood flowed, he tossed the body aside and seized another. By the time the seventh body had been drained and thrown into the corner, there was a good amount of blood in the cauldron.

Slowly Ali removed all his clothing, and stood naked.

It was then that he heard a kind of music sounding throughout the house, like the music of the sea from inside a cave, and then like echoes resounding between high mountains or the sounds that come up from a very deep well.

He listened for a moment, and then lifted the cauldron and began to pour the blood over the top of his head. It ran down his body onto the white cloth, making a design that grew bigger each second.

Once he had completed his bath of blood, he carried out the cauldron, and after dragging all the old women together into a pile, he spread the white cloth over them. Two or three still made twitching motions.

Happy at last, he turned to the mirror expecting to see himself naked and shining with wet blood.

But a man he had never seen before stood

there fully dressed, glaring at him.

Ali was beside himself with rage. How did you get in there? he bellowed. What do you want? What have I got to do to be free of all you monsters?

As he spoke, he picked up a heavy brass candlestick and hurled it at the intruder's head. The mirror shattered and the splinters showered over the floor. At the same time blood began to stream from the frame around the glass.

Ali stood perfectly still, watching.

The blood trickled and dripped from all sides of the high frame. When he glanced at the floor, he saw that each sliver of glass was red with blood.

I've killed him, he thought with satisfaction.

There was a flash of lightning, and he felt himself fall to the floor. And from where he lay he heard the roar of wind and the lash of rain.

In the midst of the storm a giant bird appeared at the window, and Ali watched as it pushed itself into the ballroom and began to move toward the pile of bodies under their bloodsoaked covering.

He saw himself seize a razor and rush at this creature. Then he saw it fall on its side, fluttering and kicking, and as it flopped around on the floor it lost not only its blood, but also its feathers. He watched it grow as naked as he was himself, and only then did he see that its body was not that of a bird, but of a frog. Then it became only a formless lump of flesh.

Now Ali found himself lying among the

bits of broken glass on the floor. The hollow music still echoed in the air, softer and much lower in pitch.

When the sound had died away into silence, he stood up, and seeing the skin on his body all caked with blood, went to clean himself.

By the time he had finished washing and dressing, it was the hour of the fjer. In another hour it would be daylight. He decided to go to the farm and sleep on the floor of the hut in the orchard.

He arrived at dawn, went into the hut, and lay down on the mat. For a while he listened to the crickets singing in the silence of the country, and it was during those moments that he determined to sell the house in the town and live at the farm. Then he fell asleep, awakening only at the end of the day.

When it was dark he set out for the city, taking four mules along with him. On arriving at his house he left them outside the door and carried a pile of sacks into the ballroom. He put each body into a sack, tied it firmly, and carried it out.

Finally he had two bodies on each of the mules, and one on the mule he rode.

He led them all back to the farm, and there in the darkness he buried the bodies of the old women along with the bloody cloth, taking care that his watchman did not see him. Then he walked back into the city and spent the night cleaning the ballroom.

The following day Ali worked with his men at the farm, and as the day passed, he began to feel happy for the first time in many months.

As he ate that evening with the workers, he chatted and joked with them as he had used to do when he was still a bachelor. The men noticed his good spirits, but said nothing.

14

That night while he slept, he found himself wandering in the desert. When he came to an oasis, he recognized it as a place where he had been before. He sat down by a pool under the palm tree and stared into the water.

Suddenly he looked up. A girl was standing beside him. When he saw her face clearly he drew back and cried out.

No! No! Not all over again!

You promised me, Ali, she murmured. You promised that after everything had happened, we could be together. Now everything has happened.

As she spoke, Ali realized that this was not Rachida, but the girl in the mirror.

She saw what he was thinking, and said: An apple is not a pear, a quince is not a grape, an orange is not a pomegranate. And I am not Rachida, even though you may think I look like her.

Rachida was beautiful, Ali said. But no more than you.

The girl smiled and sat down beside him. They spoke together for a while, and then, seeing that she suddenly seemed downcast, he questioned her.

If only you had not broken the mirror, I could have gone out that way, she said.

Ali did not understand. He drew her to him and kissed her.

Upon waking the following morning Ali was thoughtful. He understood that he could be with the girl only in his sleep because she was a prisoner in the desert.

After all, he thought, it would be enough to spend the nights with her. During the day I can work on the farm.

He did not talk much with his workers that day. As evening approached, he was beset by the fear that he might not be able to dream of the girl. There was no reason to suppose that he could.

Nevertheless, when the hour of sleep came, as soon as he had stretched out on the mat, he found himself by the pool with the girl, and she was just as he had left her that morning when he awoke.

She took him to the village in the oasis, and there he saw the man and the woman who had visited him at the farm. This time they were displeased with him.

This is not the way we understood it was to be, they told Ali. If and when our daughter married you, she was to be free and live with you at your house. Now you can be together only part of the time, and you can see her only here in the desert. What kind of marriage is that? You should not have broken the mirror.

The girl began to weep, and Ali could do nothing to comfort her in front of her parents. They, however, seeing the young people's distress, agreed to allow them to marry.

Of course he is not cured, said the woman. But at least now he is not dead.

The wedding took place a week later. It was a simple feast, and everyone in the village was there. They danced in the oasis, around a great fire of palm branches.

Each evening when he had finished working on the land with his men, Ali would eat his dinner, smoke a few pipes of kif, and go into the cabin. There in the silence he would lie down and wait for sleep to come and take him to the pool in the oasis where the girl in white sat waiting for him.